One Million Men
And Me

Kelly Starling Lyons
Illustrated by Peter Ambush

To the men of the Million Man March, with appreciation and love.

www.justusbooks.com
ISBN: 978-1-933491-07-3
Printed in China
10 9 8 7 6 5 4 3 2 1
Cataloging in Publication Data is available.

My cousin, Omari, said no girls were allowed.

But Daddy took me.

Our bus rumbled through ebony night.
My head snuggled into Daddy's warm chest

and the driver called, "Washington, D.C."

Like a quilt of moving pieces, we walked together, singing songs that made my heart dance.

We stood tall and proud as mighty oaks, the men, Daddy and me.

They came to make
changes, came to make
themselves and their
communities better.

And I was their princess,
there to see the dream of
this day come true.

I squeezed Daddy's hand as
the view stretched before
us—one millon Black men,
   one million Black kings.

Happiness glowed
in Daddy's eyes.
Tears shone too.

Daddy lifted me on his shoulders
as voices rang around us:
Sister Angelou,
    Rev. Jackson,
        Minister Farrakhan.

Men chanted.
A sea of fists thrust
toward the sky.

I looked at the faces, wrinkled and smooth— at skin a rainbow of chocolate, graham cracker brown and cream.

Daddy said they were doctors, garbage men, students, homeless people and retirees.

They came to the March to pray
and take responsibility.

Everywhere I looked, fathers and sons, friends and strangers, clasped hands in unity. Their faces filled with pride. Their hearts swelled with hope.

I held my head a little higher.

Daddy said they
missed school and
work to join in purpose
and peace.

Drums thumped.
I felt the magic.
And I held my head
a little higher.

Someone called for the men to give and they answered.

Dollars for a new future flowed
overhead, a river of green.

EXTENSION

Daddy put me down and my heart pounded as I listened to the sounds of the men all around, to the slap of hands saying hello, to the boom of laughter.

The roar of speakers echoed in my ears as powerful words traveled up to the sky and back.

I watched Daddy nod and smile at everyone we passed.

I asked if he knew them. He said no. Didn't have to. They were his brothers, here and always.

I saw signs bright with bold letters.

"I am a Man"

I am One in a Million

I saw a long pool that sparkled in the sunshine like glass.

Daddy said it was made for thinking and wishing.

I looked at the men, united and strong. I clenched my eyes as tightly as I could.

"What did you wish for, Nia?" Daddy asked when I opened them.

But I knew if I told him my wish might not come true.

So I just smiled and he understood.

We sat on the grass
as cotton candy clouds
floated above us.

And we watched the men
talking and hugging—Daddy
and me.

Then like a quilt of moving pieces, we boarded buses, trains and subways and hopped into cars all too soon.

We headed back down highways, back to Mama and my friends. I waved until my hand got tired and I snuggled my head into its special place.

But I'll always remember
the day Daddy took me
on a journey.

The day a million Black men
stood shoulder to shoulder,
the day history was made with
one million men and me.

Author's Note

When Nation of Islam leader, the Honorable Minister Louis Farrakhan, called for a Million Man March, word streaked across the nation. So many Black men spoke of the idea with hope and pride. You could hear the excitement in their voices, see it in their eyes. They would be one million men united to make the community and themselves better, to show the world who Black men were.

Men rallied at organizing meetings. Deejays announced plans on the radio. Friends and strangers asked each other, "Are you going?" Weeks before the historic day, October 16, 1995, I vowed as a journalist to be there, too.

On that peaceful Monday, I gasped as I gazed at a sea of beautiful brown faces. Black men of different ages, religious beliefs and economic backgrounds stood shoulder to shoulder. They made new friendships, pledged to strengthen Black neighborhoods and their families, prayed for peace and healing. They listened to powerful words from speakers such as Min. Farrakhan; March Director, Rev. Dr. Benjamin F. Chavis, Jr.; Rev. Jesse Jackson; Mrs. Rosa Parks; Dr. Dorothy I. Height; Dr. Maya Angelou and a young orator named Ayinde Jean-Baptiste. Men greeted the women who attended with respect and appreciation. There was peace that day and love.

Around the nation and world, millions watched the March on TV. Some people wondered what would happen when the men returned to their communities. Would the spirit of change continue? After the March, the answer was seen and felt. Black men registered to vote in record numbers. There was a spike in applications to adopt black children. Some men started new businesses and organizations, volunteered, rededicated themselves to houses of worship or attended for the first time. Others worked to make communities safer, to become better dads, husbands and role models. Assemblies inspired by the March included the Million Woman March, Million Family March and the Millions More Movement (the tenth anniversary commemoration of the Million Man March).

I went to the March to make sure the young African-American men in the community I covered had a place to tell their stories. But I had a testimony, too. So many images touched me. Then, I saw a girl walk past the Reflecting Pool clutching her daddy's hand. Her eyes, big as quarters, glittered like diamonds. She walked like a little princess among kings.

This story was inspired by the beautiful Black men and boys who stood together at the March, by that sweet girl, by everyone who made the dream of the Million Man March come true. Not long ago, I talked to a group of young people who never heard of the Million Man March. I hope this story will help change that. Like the 1963 March on Washington, we need to remember the Million Man March, a brilliant event where Black men made history.